Dare Me

Dare Me

The STEELE BROTHERS series
book 3

JENNIFER PROBST

Acknowledgements

A huge thank you to the team at Cool Gus Publishing - Bob Mayer and Jen Talty - for all of their hard work and consistent look toward the future. You help me get more quality books to my readers and that, has made all the difference!

Author's Note

I've loved writing the Steele Brother series, and when I learned my rights were returned and decided to self-publish them with additional scenes, new covers, and a brand new installment, I was excited to share with my readers.

Please note these books are different from my other contemporary romance novels. The stories are erotic, with BDSM elements such as spanking, bondage, use of toys, and other explicit sexual scenes.

I never want my readers to feel disappointed, or misled, so if erotic BDSM is not your mug of tea, please do not read these books. I've decided NOT to use a pen name because my name is my brand, and I didn't want to confuse anyone. I also love writing every type of story, exploring different genres, lengths, and want to include these books under my own brand.

Thank you for listening, thank you for reading, and as always, thank you for your support. I hope you enjoy the story!

Chapter One

*R*AFE STEELE GAZED AT his two older brothers and bit back his instinct to bolt. Of course, he held his ground like he protected his unit. Another lesson he learned from the cradle. When his brothers scented weakness, they attacked accordingly.

"You want me to what?" he asked again.

Odd how all of them seemed to belong to three different families. As the oldest, Rick always dominated both the conversation and the scene, and his resemblance to Thor, as Tara, his girlfriend phrased it, didn't hurt his image. Long golden locks, green-gold eyes, and a brutish build caused a person to think he'd stepped from a comic book. Of course, Rafe held that comment back. The last time he'd teased Rick about Thor-like powers, he almost caught a black eye. Definitely no sense of humor there.

Rome acted just as bad. He belonged in the George Clooney camp, as his girlfriend, Sloane, confided, with his buzzed prematurely gray hair, blue eyes, and a confidence and charm that made females drop their panties. As one of the best dealers in Vegas, Rome consistently threatened Rick's command. Of course, since he'd also recently fallen into the love entrapment, his domestic bliss softened him a bit. He seemed to completely agree with his brother, and that left Rafe as the focus of this intervention.

The other men exchanged knowing glances.

"We want you to book a date through FANTA-C," Rick said.

Rafe struggled to make sense of his words over the familiar casino noises of ringing slots, heavy drinking, and loud rivalry.

"The place you both ended up meeting the loves of your life?"

Rick nodded. Rome looked suspicious, wondering if he was poking fun at his brothers' sudden slide into commitment. He kind of was.

Rafe gave a snort of laughter and ordered a shot of Jack Daniels. "You're fucking nuts. Both of you. I have no intention or desire to settle down."

Rick huffed. "We're not saying the date is going to turn into more than one night. Yeah, we got lucky, but it was coincidence. Both of us agree you've been a bit out of it since you moved to Vegas. You keep to yourself. Don't date much anymore. Something's up."

He waved his brothers' concern away and tossed back his shot in one stinging swallow. Surprised by their insight, he admitted he'd been restless and agitated since moving across the US to join them in their legacy of dealing cards. He'd tried living in Atlantic City when he returned from Afghanistan, but the local newshounds battered him on a daily basis. When the women started camping out to make up ruses to bed a real-time hero, he packed up his belongings and moved on. He craved a clean slate and a place where he could get back to what he loved. Dealing cards. Alone. By choice.

His brothers thought he suffered from war stress—specifically post-traumatic stress disorder. Sure, he'd experienced some wicked nightmares, but his uneasiness and secrecy had nothing to do with his military past.

If only they knew the truth.

An intriguing idea skipped through his mind with various scenarios. "Tell me again how this whole thing works."

Rome slid a business card across the table. The card was black and gold, with FANTA-C scrawled in embossed lettering on the front. On the back, a phone number was listed. "You call that number. Use my name as your referral, because Rick already used his referral for me. Fill out your paperwork, and if they find you a match, you get to enjoy one perfect night."

He frowned, turning the card around in his hand. A weird shiver raced down his spine. "This isn't some sex club that's illegal, is it? Cause I'm not into that shit."

Rome gave a suffering sigh. "No, we're not into that shit either, dude."

Rick jumped in. "A friend told me about the agency. Some want sex, some don't. It's whatever you need. And you're not guaranteed a match. They only fit you with a candidate that wants the same exact things you do."

"Hmm. Interesting."

Rome elbowed him in the ribs. "Why do I think you have something wicked planned? Probably involving a pretty sub tied to the bed."

"Like Sloane?" Rafe asked.

Immediately, Rome's face darkened at the mention of his sex life. "Back off, bro."

Rafe released a shout of laughter. "Priceless, man. I'm just joking around—you know I adore Sloane." But Rome's assumption that he practiced as a Dom punched his gut. His two older brothers were experienced in BDSM, and long-term Dominants who finally found a committed submissive. Rafe had never confessed the truth of his real desires. They'd never understand, so he continued to let them think he was also a Dominant.

"And this is completely confidential?" he asked.

"Yes. Oh, you have to burn the card after you call. It's protocol," Rick said.

Rafe held up the card. "Then how'd you get this?"

"Once the match is complete, they send you one card for referral."

Rafe laughed. "Doesn't this seem like a lot of work to get a perfect date?"

His brothers shared a meaningful glance. "It's worth it," they both said together.

Damn, this got more interesting by the moment. They weren't the type to believe in mysterious hook-ups that turn into love, so maybe he'd give FANTA-C a shot. He'd get his brothers off his back, and finally be able to act out one of his secret sexual fantasies. No one ever had to know.

"You paying for it?" he asked.

Rick shook his head and took another swig of beer. "Bastard."

"Well, are you?"

"Yeah, we're paying for it. Consider this our housewarming present a few months late."

Rafe grinned. "Fine, I'll call.

***

Summer Preston ordered a second shot of tequila and watched the show on stage at *Strip It*. The sexy lyrics of Prince's *Get Off* pounded through the air while the stripper gyrated her hips and ripped off her leather vest. Her naked breasts spilled out and the crowd screamed. Her skin glittered with silver sparkles, and she flung her whip toward her audience with a teasing flick that made them go wild. Summer narrowed her eyes thoughtfully on the instrument that provided both pleasure and pain. Hmm, would it be too much for the first night?

Yeah. She'd skip the whips and flogger. *At least for tonight.*

She scanned the entrance. Excitement jumped in her belly. They'd both agreed meeting in the suite would be postponed until they decided if they were compatible. When her cousin told her about FANTA-C and told her to call the number, she'd been doubtful. Summer didn't do one night encounters, or believe in the perfect date. Over the years, her luck with finding the correct match on her own proved...difficult. Most men switched from arousal to horror when they caught a glance of her leather catsuit and domineering growl. Pete had lunged for the door so fast he'd literally tripped on the rug and fell face first.

Awkward.

She shook her head at the memory. Nope, she'd suggested meeting at the strip club first to make sure they clicked. She'd been specific in her requirements, and thought of this as her first real learning experience in the BDSM world. Hell, maybe the reality wouldn't even come close to her fantasies and she could go back to normal vanilla sex. After all, her reputation and her image fed the girl next-door persona. Her few visits to a BDSM club scared the crap out of her, and her forays into toys and certain internet sites never snagged a willing partner. At least she learned the importance of safety and equipment, but never experienced her own personal sub for the night. She needed to face the truth: strong, dominant males attracted her in the real world, but she craved a man's surrender in the bedroom. That combination rarely existed. The possibility of experiencing such a scene for one night tempted her. Pricey, but worth it.

So, she'd called the number and burned the card. Two weeks later, they found a match.

If he showed.

She tapped a scarlet red fingernail on the bar.

And waited.

Chapter Two

RAFE PUSHED HIS WAY INTO the club and took stock of the surroundings. Only a few months in Vegas proved the city boasted the best strip clubs in the country. The unique mix of class, club scene, and nakedness pulled in record crowds. The three main bars were strategically placed around the room. One snaked around the perimeter of the stage, and the others huddled in dark corners, which lent to the aura of sensuality and privacy. The catwalk glittered with vivid neon colors and sparkles, and flashed in time to whatever music currently played. Skimpily dressed waiters and waitresses balanced trays of cocktails, as they shifted around onlookers watching the trio of half-clothed women doing a mock up of the *Flashdance* skit. When water splashed the front rows, cheers rang through the air. Two dance floors on the second level looked over the stage, and catered to the club crowd.

Damn, he loved Vegas. He headed toward the bar in the far back, where they'd agreed to meet. He'd been impressed with her rendezvous choice, agreeing the suite was too personal for an introduction. A sensual feast of visual and physical stimuli, *Strip It* urged sexual explorations to the fullest. He hoped the scene proved a good precursor to his evening.

He only had a general description of his date, choosing to forego the photo, as he wanted to be surprised. He relied on two factors only. She sat at the corner left barstool and had blonde hair. He expected a sexual vixen dressed in leather with a kick ass personality.

Instead, his gaze cut straight to an angel.

Crap.

She was all-wrong.

The woman sat at the bar with a shot at her elbow, her jeans and simple white T-shirt fading into the crowd of peacocks mingling around her. His heart sank. A Dominatrix? Impossible. He'd eat her up in one bite and she'd be screaming for the door. Fighting his temper, he clenched his jaw. Attractive, yes. Her shimmering white-blonde hair gleamed like a halo in a ponytail. Big, china blue eyes dominated her softly curved face. A generous bow curved her lower lip and she had a killer body, evident in the perfect hourglass waist, small, high breasts with perky nipples, and a luscious ass sitting atop the red leather barstool. He studied her white Keds and almost groaned in defeat. Not even a spiked heel in sight. He was screwed.

And not in a good way.

FANTA-C had flopped. Now what was he going to do? With a deep, resigned breath, he closed the distance between them.

"Summer?" His tongue stumbled over her name, the image of a sweet, sunny girl next door-type adding to his disgust.

She stared up at him with frank appraisal. She didn't answer for a while. Surprise coursed through him as those baby blues started at the top of his head, lowered to his chest, and scanned his arms. Then dropped.

He hardened when her hot gaze caressed him between the legs, and he shifted uneasily. *Who the hell is this woman?*

Completing her inspection, she nodded her approval. "Rafe, I assume?" Her voice was cool. "You'll do fine."

His mouth snapped closed. "Uh, glad to hear it." A short silence settled between them and she made no move to speak. Just lifted the shot glass and tipped it, then slid her tongue over her plump lower lip to grab the last drop of liquid. He imagined the sting of the tequila hot down her throat, chased by the tart lime she sucked on. His cock strained to full attention. God, how firm would her lips grasp it? Sexual attraction jumped between them like a live wire. He just needed to confirm she was strong enough to handle him. He motioned toward the two empty shot glasses. "Potent stuff. Wouldn't want you drunk on our first date."

The wicked grin she shot him transformed her face from angel to Eve. "Don't worry, I have a high tolerance." His gaze roamed over her petite frame and he lifted a brow. She laughed. "Let's share a drink and decide if we want to take this to the suite. Beer?"

"Jack Daniels."

"Nice." She lifted her arm for the bartender. He let her order the drinks, deciding to hold back further judgment until he got a better reading. So far, the woman fascinated the hell out of him. They clinked glasses. "To a memorable night," she toasted. The shot disappeared down her throat without a flinch and she leaned forward. "What do you think?"

His lips quirked in amusement. "About what?"

"About me. About us. About tonight."

He studied her from over his shot glass. "You're not what I expected when I signed on for this."

Instead of being offended, she nodded glumly. "You expected leather and heels, huh? I'm more like the wholesome girl next door. Is it the Keds?"

He sputtered with laughter. "Yeah, the sneakers didn't help. Look, this is new to me. I come from a background where I yell jump, and a bunch of men ask 'how high.' It won't be easy for me to just snap to attention, and I don't want to intimidate you."

She raised her chin. Pure challenge sparked in her eyes. "I understand, and this is all new to me, too. That's why I didn't want to meet you at a club dressed to the nines. I can't help that I look like this. This is who I am day to day. I like a man to buy me dinner and open the door. I love knowing he's stronger than me, can kick some major ass, and won't back down from a good, old-fashioned bar room fight. But in the bedroom, I want to be in charge. At least, I think I do."

He sucked in a breath at her honesty. *Hmm, a bit of a spitfire in a nice, neat package.* Isn't that what he craved? A woman who wouldn't be afraid to tell him what she wanted, and what she wanted him to do? He was sick to death of being a leader every waking moment. Domination came easily to him, always had. In school, his classmates gravitated toward him for captain; he'd always been picked by his teachers to lead group discussions. When he joined the military, his natural confidence and quest for perfection pushed him to the head of the class. He'd risen quickly up the ranks, until he found himself in the scorching desert, leading a brigade of men in war.

Every order equaled life or death, with no room for error.

His decision not to re-up changed the game. He went back to Atlantic City with an open mind, and enjoyed getting back to his main love—dealing cards. But when a long line of women with endless needs began draining his energy instead of fueling it, he knew something was wrong. His mind tired of doing all the work, and his body began to suffer. When a gorgeous woman who wanted to be subservient begged for his command and his cock never hardened, he'd gone into hibernation mode.

Maybe he needed Summer Preston.

Maybe.

He raked his gaze over her figure. Tipped back his glass and swallowed the burning liquid. "Let's go."

She shot to her feet and pressed a room key in his hands. "Room 310. Venetian.

Give me a fifteen-minute head start."

He nodded and watched her disappear into the crowd.

Chapter Three

*S*UMMER PACED THE LUSHLY carpeted suite and tried to ignore the flutter in her tummy. In a minute, she'd open her door to an overpowering, sexy male predator who she'd try to subjugate to her every sexual whim.

Yeah, right.

She pushed the doubt firmly out of her mind. Rafe Steele was unexpected. She'd always had a weakness for the tall, dark, and handsome type, but the man put them all to shame. Sinfully inky eyes promised a quick trip to heaven, and dark curls begged a woman to thrust her fingers in deep and hang on. His face was all rough planes and angles—sharp cheekbones, a crooked nose, shaggy dark brows, and an unshaven chin. His mouth held a sensual, almost cruel curve that stripped away any pretty boy looks and made a man look twice and a woman salivate.

His body appeared rock hard and unforgiving. Even in his simple charcoal button down shirt, and jeans, the muscles rippled beneath the fabric. She guessed he topped six feet, but it was the sheer dominance of his presence that pressed upon her. An aura of command when he spoke. He struck her as a man used to being in charge.

She bet women lined up to do his bidding. Yet, he hadn't backed off when she'd adopted a forceful tone in their conversation. In fact, his dark eyes flashed with a gleam of interest. And lust.

A knock sounded on the door.

Showtime.

She took a deep breath and let him in.

Her throat tightened. Dear God, the man practically exuded sex. Even his scent screamed animal mating, like smoke, musk, and earth rolled together. He stalked into her room as though he owned it. His clothes seemed to bend to his will, the fabric surrendered to his carved chest and molded to his powerful thighs and ass.

His shocked stare told her she'd done her job well. Satisfaction flared, along with a hint of feminine power. The girl next door had turned into a vixen, and she relished every moment of enveloping sexual authority. The skin-tight leather cat suit with heels transformed her from sweet teacher to badass.

She pursed her lips and studied him, making a circling motion with her finger.

"Turn around."

One brow shot up. His face tightened with a mingling of emotions. Arrogance. Denial.

Excitement.

Yes, he loved taking orders from a woman, as much as she loved giving them. The problem centered on his acceptance and trust of her as a mistress. She ached to give him what he craved, but first he'd have to submit to his own dark desires. A man used to control and leadership in all other areas of his world would be hard pressed to easily accept such a switch of power even if he wanted to.

"What?"

He looked as if he didn't recognize her from the strip club and had entered the Twilight Zone. Satisfaction coursed through her at his response. "Tonight you will address me as Summer. I have not earned your trust yet to be called Mistress. The rules are simple. You obey my every order without question. If you refuse, you will be punished. Your body belongs to me until dawn breaks. Are we clear?"

He nodded.

Her voice snapped like a whiplash. "I didn't hear you."

"Yes. Summer." His instant response surged heat through her veins. A tight ache settled between her thighs.

"Very good. You will need a safe word. Think of one you'll easily remember. If you use your safe word, the scene will immediately stop. We will decide if the evening can continue afterward. What is your word?"

"Blackjack."

"Blackjack, it is. Now, turn around in a full circle. Slowly."

The simple test confirmed her assumptions. He obeyed, his muscles tight with tension. He shot her a look hinting he'd do what she said, but she also knew restraints would definitely be needed for the night.

"Your body is incredible. I can't wait until you're able to pleasure me. But we're not ready for that yet. Strip."

He blinked. Refused to move. She closed the distance between them with two long strides and met his gaze head on. "I don't like to repeat myself." Her voice was icy. "Take off your clothes so I can see

14

every gorgeous inch that belongs to me. Hesitate again and you'll be punished."

He jolted as if awakening from a dream, and removed his clothes.

She caught her breath. Wide shoulders. Carved muscles, broad chest. Cut abs. The line of a wicked scar ran down his ribs and disappeared into a swirl of dark hair. A heavy erection jutted forward and strained against his black boxers. His thumbs hooked on the elastic and paused. She narrowed her eyes in warning. Then he pushed the fabric down his thighs and stepped out of his underwear.

He stood with his feet apart, hands on hips. She took in the raw male glory. His cock rose to full attention. Her mouth watered and she ached to dip her head and suck on the long, thick length. Her hot gaze traveled over every inch of his body and she nodded in approval then ran her tongue along her lower lip. His cock twitched in response to the gesture....

"Beautiful." She walked around him for a full inspection. Her fingers clenched at the sight of his tight ass, imagining how he'd jerk in response to a paddling. Pressing her breasts against his back, she placed her hands on his shoulders and stroked him. His muscles jumped under her touch. "I'm already wet," she whispered in his ear. Her teeth nipped at his earlobe. "Would you like a taste?"

"Yes, Summer."

His voice hissed and she gave a low laugh. Running her hands down his arms, she squeezed his biceps. Her hips pushed against his ass. "Not yet. I want to play with your body for a while. You are not to touch me until I give you permission. Do you understand?"

"Yes."

"Very good." She slid her arms around his waist and splayed her palms over his chest. His heart thundered against her hand, and a fine sheen of sweat beaded his skin. *Oh, yeah.* He liked her attention, but how would he handle not being in charge? She dug her nails into his abs and kicked his feet apart with one black heel until his legs spread wide. He locked down his body to avoid moving and his breath came in heavy gasps. Murmuring approval, she drifted her palms downward and played with the nest of hair at the base of his cock, running one finger down the ridged length, up and down, never applying more than a hint of pressure.

He bit back a groan.

Her fingers circled the tip, spreading around the bead of moisture that dripped. Slowly, she cupped and stroked his balls.

His temper exploded.

With a curse, he spun and pulled her into his arms. His mouth lowered to take hers, but she took a quick step back, and grabbed his balls in a merciless grip. She allowed her face to reflect her cold displeasure. Shock blazed back at her and his cock jumped in response.

"Remove your hands." His arms dropped to his side. She shook her head in mockery. "Not enough control, I see. The rules are simple. Your body is mine for my pleasure. You obey my commands, and you don't touch me unless I give permission. Since you can't listen on your own, I'll need to give you a little help." A slight twist of her hand exerted more pressure and he winced. "Don't move." Releasing him, she walked to the small bureau and pulled out a pair of leather handcuffs from the top drawer.

"No fucking way."

Her brow arched. "Yes fucking way. You proved you can't be trusted on your own. This will make sure you keep your hands to yourself."

"I'll obey next time."

"Yes, you will," she said. "Because I'll make sure of it. Follow me."

With his feet rooted to the ground, they'd reached a turning point. He'd either take the leap and put himself in her hands, or stalk out the door with his pride intact. Of course, pride made a cold bed partner and ranked unnecessary in the pursuit of pleasure. Conflict flickered in his dark eyes as he processed his options. Summer gave him the only gift she owned. Her truth.

"Aren't you as tired of running as I am?" she asked softly. She extended her hand and waited.

He stiffened and glared at the handcuffs before slowly sauntering over to grasp her hand. Heat and comfort radiated from his fingers straight to her heart. An age-old connection sizzled and settled between them in a steady hum. She led him to the bedroom toward the far wall of the suite, where she'd already had certain equipment installed at her request per FANTA-C. The bedroom boasted a Tuscan feel, with rich gold, browns, and burgundy. The bed held piles of pillows against an ornate oak headboard. The cream satin sheets beckoned and glistened under the last rays of the dying sun that sneaked through the Venetian blinds. With one last moment of hesitation, he surrendered his hands. She fastened the handcuffs, checking the fit and his comfort. She grabbed the chain from the drawer, attached it to the hook that hung discreetly from the ceiling, and connected the cuffs. He sucked in his breath, but she never glanced at him or hesitated, just pulled the chain up and connected it so his hands stretched over his head. She released some slack inch by inch until satisfied. "How does that feel?"

A beat passed. "Uncomfortable."

"Painful?"

"No."

"Good." She'd targeted enough discomfort to allow him the opportunity to concentrate on his body, and not what he should be doing or thinking. She reached under the bed, took out a foot spreader, and positioned it between his legs. After a quick check of the equipment, she stood back to admire the naked man in front of her.

A slow, satisfied smile curved her lips. "Perfect. Let's begin."

* * *

Holy shit.

In a matter of minutes, he found himself naked, spread-eagled, and tied up before a female he'd never met before tonight. *I've lost my freaking mind.*

The last incident in Afghanistan flashed before his vision. Their transporter had been attacked. As bullets rained over them and he'd shot back, sweat dripping in his eyes, adrenalin pumping, sand bursting up in clouds so he didn't know what the hell he aimed at, he'd reached a turning point. When Ben was cut down, his leg shot to pieces, Rafe had needed to make a life-changing decision in a moment. He'd dived into the danger zone to bring his friend back to safety and hoped life without a limb wouldn't be as bad as dying.

Right now, right here, with this woman before him, he hit another turning point.

He craved a bit of secret Dom/sub play, but never believed he'd experience a full-blown episode. His senses buzzed in vivid neon colors, riding the edge of pain and pleasure. Since coming back from the war, he'd never felt so completely alive. In touch with his body and completely present. Focused only on the woman before him who was about to rock his world.

Jesus, she looked like a different woman. Her face still held the appeal of the girl-next-door, but now she emanated a seductive power that gripped him by the balls and squeezed him as hard as her fingers had. High, perfectly formed breasts played a game of hide and seek behind tight leather. Her nipples grazed the edge of the corset, about to pop out with her next deep breath. Skintight pants left nothing to the imagination and cupped her ass, clearly outlining the delta between her thighs. Each time she took a step, the heels forced her to balance, pushing her hips forward, and back in a feminine swing, Eve couldn't have perfected better. Each thrust beckoned with a promise. If he hung on.

He'd figured she'd call it quits the moment he fought her. He hadn't expected her to twist his balls, or the crazy pain/pleasure that stiffened his dick at her complete demand of submission. His mind emptied of all other thoughts than getting to touch her, thrust inside of her, see her completely naked. He figured he'd take anything she gave if she'd allow him just a taste.

"Hmm, very nice." She grasped his cock and slid down from tip to the base. He shuddered and pulled on the cuffs, but the movement cramped and burned his shoulders and neck. He raised almost on tiptoe and stretched his body. Her touch skittered over his skin and twisted the discomfort into excitement. "I want to know more about you," she purred like Catwoman. "We're going to play one of my favorite games. I'll ask you something and you answer as honestly as possible. If you give me the truth, I'll give you a present. Lie to me, and you'll be punished. Do you understand?"

"Yes, Summer."

"Very good." She continued touching him with light strokes—his hip, his stomach, his nipple. Each teasing flutter fisted his gut with anticipation; until he worried, he'd spurt all over her like a freaking horn-dog teenager. He used all of his military training to lock down his brain and control his body. No way in hell, he'd explode before he pushed inside of her. She picked the wrong man to play that game with.

As if she sensed his thoughts, she lifted one of her hands and he held his breath as her pink tongue licked her palm. She grasped his erection. And squeezed. He bucked at the damp heat.

"Stop thinking," she commanded. "You'll do what I ask, not what you think you have to. How long were you in the military?"

"Ten years. Joined at eighteen."

She rubbed both hands up and down his cock, her thumb massaging the tip, keeping him distracted. "Where were you stationed?"

"Afghanistan."

"Tell me about it."

He blinked, reaching for some answer to her strange question, but she continued stroking. "Uh, what do you want to know?"

"Describe how it felt."

He groaned when she scratched his sensitive balls with her fingernails. "Hot. Dusty. Had sand in my ass from the first day, and the grit doesn't wash off your skin no matter how much you bathe. You learn not to trust anyone but your team since any resident can turn on you in a heartbeat. Children included."

She released him and disappeared behind him. He tensed. Her breath ran hot over his back and one sharp nail traced the line of his spine to stop at the base before tracing the line of his ass cheeks. He closed his eyes and pulled at the chains, wanting out of there, yet he had nowhere to go.

"Tell me your worst memory in Afghanistan."

Her finger teased the tight hole between his cheeks. He concentrated on keeping his breathing steady, his heartbeat under control and played his usual game that kept him grounded. Start with one thousand and count backward, slow, and steady. No way in hell, he'd share secrets with a one-night stand. No way in hell, she'd make him.

"Nothing stands out. One crappy day was the same as the rest."

A sharp slap rang through the air. His left ass cheek tightened and heat burned his skin, but before he recovered, she bit down and the other cheek stung like a son of a bitch. Her hand slid around and grasped his cock, pumping up and down in a steady rhythm and the dual shock of pain melded to pleasure. Her tongue soothed the sting on his ass. With his head swimming, he tried to keep his brain sharp in order to dodge her questions, but his body didn't give a shit. He cursed viciously.

"Don't lie to me, it'll piss me off. Let's backtrack. Were you in charge of anyone?"

"Yes, five men."

"Were they close friends?"

"Yes."

"Did everyone get out alive?"

The repetitive questions came fast. His mind throbbed in time with the demands of his body to come. "No."

He descended into his own personal hell, fighting with lust, need, and crappy memories he didn't want to emerge. Then she appeared in front of him. She'd loosened her corset and bared her breasts. Two ruby red nipples poked out and begged for his mouth.

"Who died?"

He gritted his teeth. She reached out and slapped his cock. A few drops of cum moistened the tip and he groaned. "Ben."

"How did he die?"

"Fuck you."

The last ditch effort at sanity broke from his lips. She smiled and knelt before him. Her hands rubbed her nipples and he stared helplessly at the luscious fruit a few inches away, yet unable to touch. The final threads of control frayed.

"I'm going to take your cock into my mouth and suck. You are not allowed to come. Do you understand me?"

"Yes."

She opened her lips and slid her tongue up and over him. His heart stopped, sputtered, and pounded so hard the sound roared in his ears. She rolled the tip of her tongue round and round, licking with delicate motions. He jerked in the heavenly wet heat and yanked at his restraints. His knees shook. The numbers swam foggily in his vision but he fought for composure and tried to count again.

She pulled her mouth away with a slight popping noise. "How did Ben die?"

"Ambushed. We took cover but he got hit and his leg was blown off."

"What did you do?"

"Nothing."

The witch actually smiled. She bathed her index finger with her tongue. Her hot breath blew on his throbbing cock, and she trailed the same finger slowly between his cheeks, teasing the opening of his anus. Horror and a raging arousal licked him like fire. "Liar," she said softly. One finger thrust into his ass.

"Fuck!" The delicious pressure shoved him toward the edge of orgasm. She worked the finger like a magician until his body practically wept for more.

"What happened when Ben got hit?"

"I asked Tim to cover me and I went to get him. Dragged him out of the scene." He panted. With her other hand, she lifted his erection, swirling her fingers under the sensitive base, around his balls, spreading the moisture of her mouth.

"Did you get shot?" she asked.

"No. Everyone said it was a miracle."

Pain and desire melded until one became indistinct from the other. The memory pierced him clear and sharp. Before it had always been a dull throbbing echo that never seemed to go away. She battered him with questions, and still she worked him, never easing the pressure of her finger in his ass, or her tongue and lips on his cock.

"Did you save him?"

"That day I did. He died at the hospital later. The whole thing was a waste. Just another day of waste."

"Was that your worst memory?"

Her gaze delved deep and grabbed him by the throat. An endless depth of blue churned with emotion and demanded his truth. The walls he'd built trembled and broke in a pile of rubble around him. His body screamed and shook for release, for her permission to come. He dug in and gave it to her. "No, my worst memory was the day I got that fucking medal. The Silver Star. For being a damned hero." He waited for her revulsion, anger, and resentment.

Instead, he only met her understanding and empathy. And want.

"Very good. Now, you may come in my mouth."

Her head dipped and she took him deep to the back of her throat in one swift gulp. She sucked hard, her tongue swirling around with the perfect pressure. A cry ripped from his lips. Her teeth gently scraped the underside of his dick; she thrust a second finger in his anus, and he let go.

The climax ripped through him and he screamed her name, bucking and coming in her slick, satin heat. His toes arched and his head exploded in sensory overload as every muscle released tension. Mini convulsions wracked him from side to side, and she took all of him, massaging, and then crooning to him softly. Drained emotionally and physically, he slumped against the handcuffs and heard her murmur his name. Time slowed and blurred. He caught the sweet scent of soap on her damp hands as she freed him from his restraints and rubbed his sore muscles. Settling him on the bed, she pressed kisses to his forehead as he lay against the cool sheets and let her bathe him with a damp washcloth. He basked in a cocoon of warmth and safety he'd never experienced before, after the most powerful orgasm of his life. In the comforting darkness, he surrendered while held within strong, feminine arms.

Chapter Four

*S*UMMER BLINKED AWAY THE tears that threatened and she bit her lip to ground herself. The man beside her roused. How would he react after the depth of their emotional scene? In a matter of hours, Rafe Steele had given her more intimacy and passion than she'd ever experienced. His strength humbled her. She shook with the need to belong to him completely, to have him fill her aching pussy.

She smoothed back a loose dark curl from his brow with a shaky hand. Would he hate her? Would he blame her for forcing him to tell his most private secrets? And could she blame him? She'd played hardball and reached for things that most women didn't try to accomplish for months. Vulnerability turned a man vicious, and she might fall victim.

His eyes opened.

She sucked in a breath at the swirl of emotion in his gaze. Recognition. Lust. Anger. Knowledge. The clock ticked. Her heart squeezed with terror at the idea of him walking away before dawn.

"Summer?"

"Yes?"

"Why are you still wearing clothes?"

She looked down at her half naked body and burst out laughing. "I got distracted." Warmth pumped through her veins and flooded to the center of her thighs. Her nipples swelled to full attention. "Besides, I want you to take them off."

He sat up, gloriously naked and tousled. "Thank God. That outfit is driving me fucking nuts."

Still grinning, she slid off the bed in one quick motion. "In a moment. I want you to drink some water."

"Anything stronger?"

"Water first."

"Yes, ma'am." Her fingers itched to smack his ass, but she loved the dual edge of dominance and subjugation he teetered on. He'd never take a backseat in life or in public. The idea he'd do it in the privacy of the bedroom cranked her lust to a whole new level.

She brought over two glasses of ice water and watched him drink. Satisfied he was properly hydrated, she poured two fingers of Jack Daniels for both of them and settled on the bed. The scent of man, musk, and arousal rose to her nostrils She studied his face carefully, but no resentment or embarrassment glimmered. "How do you feel?"

"Like I had the best orgasm of my life." His eyes darkened further. "Like I want to do it again, but this time thrusting between your thighs instead of your mouth."

She smiled. Damn, his sense of humor and honesty blew her away. "Me, too." He shook his head as if refusing to utter more thoughts. "Tell me what you're thinking."

"I can't believe I shared all that crap with you," he muttered. "Even my brothers don't know."

"I'm not surprised. Men don't spend too much time analyzing their emotions. Women wallow, and men push it aside and get on with their life. The problem is when the stuff begins to blister."

"Are you a shrink?" he asked suspiciously.

She laughed. "No. I'm an elementary school teacher."

"I knew it. Pegged you for a teacher or a librarian from the first." Questions whirled in his eyes and she waited for him to ask. "So, how does this work? Do I get to ask questions or is this just a one-man show?"

She raised a brow at his tone, secretly enjoying his masculine edge. "I have nothing to hide. If I insist on your honesty at all times, I'm certainly not holding back with you. I'll answer any questions you have."

"How did a nice elementary school teacher get hooked up with a one-night stand?"

She sighed. "I've always craved dominance in the bedroom. I was raised to believe women took a backseat to men. You know, allow them their full right to be in charge at all times. My mom tried to teach me the proper ways to make a man happy. Basically, do whatever he asks and everything he expects." The memories cut deep as she remembered her parents' own marriage. When her father asked his wife to jump, she asked how high. Summer would have been fine if he'd made her mother happy, but only rage and resentment filled the woman up, pushing away everything good. Including love for her only daughter. "My parents insisted I live up to certain ideals. Church on Sundays. Volunteer programs on weekends. I pursued a teaching degree under their watchful eye, and they even set me up with the man they expected me to marry. They were concerned I grow up with old-fashioned virtue and not become a slut of society."

He shook his head in amazement. "Hardcore. Why can't I imagine you just going along with their plan?"

"They were my parents. I assumed I needed to do what I was told. Most of the time, I enjoyed my life, but not when they focused on Andrew, the local pastor. It was the first time I disagreed with them."

"What happened?"

"Let's just say they weren't thrilled when I informed them their precious Andrew couldn't get it up in the bedroom."

He winced. "Ouch."

"Yep. They threw me out of the house and called me a whore." She shrugged. "I crashed at a friend's house and built my own life. A life I wanted, including sex."

"Do you ever talk to your parents?"

Sadness leaked through her. She refused to hide behind the wall, and allowed him to see it all. "I call them on a regular basis. Sometimes they talk to me. Once I even visited, but they only wanted to show off Andrew's new wife and baby boy. I didn't stay too long. Somehow, they're the only ones in my life who can make me feel dirty."

"I'm sorry." Rafe's words reached out in warm comfort, his husky voice washing over her in a healing massage.

"Thanks. So, back to the original question, I did some experimenting with different types of men but always left unsatisfied. Each time I tried to dominate a scene, they'd freak out. My last ex called me a head case and told me I needed therapy."

"He was an asshole. Probably afraid to listen to what you needed. Did you ever try out any BDSM clubs?"

"I went once for an orientation and learned some basics. I practiced safety with my sub and learned simple equipment. But I made no connections there, and the public scene was too much for me. At least for now. I wanted to explore in a private setting, with someone I can trust. A good friend referred me to FANTA-C and I grabbed the opportunity. When they called and told me they'd found a match, I was excited to have a night of experimentation on my own terms."

"And here we are."

She grinned at his bad boy wink. "Yes, here we are." Her fingers clenched. "What about you? What are you looking for?"

She gave him credit. He only looked uncomfortable for a moment, then pushed past and told her the truth. "I've always felt different. I grew up with three brothers who were dominant, so I never questioned that was the route for me. But I felt strangled. They already had my future mapped out—finish college, go to dealer school, and join them in Atlantic City with my pop. Poker is in the blood. But I was sick of being in their shadow and craved to make my own way. So, when I turned eighteen I joined the military. I went overseas pretty quickly because of the war. Really pissed off my family."

"Did they end up supporting your decision?"

"Yes. Once they understood I'd made up my mind, they backed me all the way. I've never regretted joining. Hell, basic training alone kicked my ass. I challenged myself, and I made friends I'll never forget." Pain ravaged his face. "Other than Ben, everyone else got out alive, but the transition is freaking crazy. Nightmares. Wondering why I'm spending time deciding on lunch when people were dying. A tire blew out on the highway once and I almost flew off the road to dive for cover. Messes with your head. I never spoke about it, and my family never asked. Eventually, I did go to dealer school and began my career. On my terms."

"When did you realize you have sub tendencies?"

He gave a short laugh. "When the best sex I had came from a woman I dated who got pissed. She started getting physical, ordering me around, and I became hard as a rock. I wanted more. Unfortunately, it never went much further after that."

"You never tried to experiment? Talk to anyone?"

He snorted. "Honey, my brothers would eat me up alive if they even guessed. They're experienced Dominants. I can't imagine the crap I'd get if they found out I take orders in the bedroom. Most women fall at my feet, ready to roll over when I ask, all because I received a fucking medal for leadership I didn't deserve. If it got out I showed up at a club as a sub, I'd be done. I consider tonight a present to myself. Get it out of my system."

She arched a brow at his terminology of his sexual preferences as an *it*. Yes, she knew what he meant. But she craved a mate who could satisfy her in the bedroom. Who cared anymore about her reputation or what society considered abnormal or normal? She wanted a man to take care of—to command and give everything she was—for his complete trust. No more hiding. When dawn rose, he'd go back to his life with its rigid rules, and maybe someday strangle under its chokehold. Not her. First, her parents, then society chose her path. Now, she'd choose on her own, but in the light of day, on her own terms.

He'd forced her to admit what she really needed, and she'd never deny herself again. If she needed to find the proper club, she would. If she needed to reach out for contacts and people involved in this lifestyle, she'd find them.

She looked at the man on the bed and a strange sadness and longing rose in her throat. Already, a strong bond had been formed, emotionally and physically. She ached to learn more, to strip him bare and give him the most immense pleasure of his life. But he wasn't ready.

She only had him until dawn.

"Must be nice to have everything under control." He shuddered and she caught the gleam of arousal in his eyes. "Let's see how well you do with some boundaries." She licked her lips as she noted his instant hard on. "But first, a kiss. Show me how much you want me. You're only allowed to touch my lips. Keep your hands to your sides."

Eagerness leapt in his gaze. He leaned forward and twisted his hands in the tangled sheets in an effort to keep still, but he did as told and carefully fit his mouth over hers.

A sluggish heat pierced her with sweet longing as his taste swamped her—stinging liquor and hot male need. As if treasuring every moment, he sipped from her lips, nibbling on the lower one in a strong measure of control, teasing the seam with his tongue. Slowly, she opened to him, and he pushed through.

Mine.

The word pounded in her head like a mantra. She fought her need to possess and allowed him full access, as his tongue explored every dark hidden cave, and plunged in over and over, fucking her mouth in perfect rhythm. The earthy scent of him filled her head, and her control slipped under her lust for more. She shuddered for his touch. Pulling away, she stared into his eyes. In a ragged, husky voice, she said, "Very good. You may touch my breasts. But not with your mouth."

"Thank you, Summer."

His words pleased her, and his big hands cupped her breasts, massaging in rough circles. Her flesh swelled to meet him and her nipples tightened. She loved the contrast between her fair skin and his olive tones. He used his thumbs to roughly tweak her nipples, scraping a nail over one tight bud. Heat lanced straight down her belly and pulsed between her thighs. God help her, she wasn't as in control as she hoped. She craved release just from his hands on her naked skin. At that rate, he'd own all the control.

An idea nibbled on the fringe of her mind. He needed another lesson in discipline. Perhaps her orgasm could introduce him to a whole new pleasure? "You've been very good," she said. "I'd like you to kneel in the middle of the bedroom for me now."

"What?"

His obvious confusion cleared her head and she drew her brows together in warning. "Not another word. Don't question me or I won't let you come. Do you understand?"

Pure mutiny carved lines on his face. A beat passed and she waited. "Yes, I understand." He rose from the bed and knelt on the mocha-colored carpet.

She squirmed at the sight of the rippling muscles in his upper thighs and ass. God, she wanted him. "Very nice. Spread your legs wider. Now lock your hands behind your back. Beautiful. You may watch as I undress."

Heat sizzled in his gaze. She peeled off her thigh high boots, unzipped the leather pants, and wriggled them down over her hips to stand naked in front of him. Her bare pussy leaked with her arousal. She heard the quick intake of his breath, and gloried in the fact that she pleased him. Carefully, she slipped her boots back on. The soft leather caressed the sensitive flesh of her inner thighs. A few drops of pre-cum glistened on the tip of his cock, and he leaned forward to rub it against the carpet, moaning under the friction.

She lifted one spiked heel and dug it into his upper thigh. He hissed at the sharp pain, but when his gaze flicked to her open folds in full view, his muscles locked down. "Straighten up and link your hands behind your back," she said. "You will sit there while I pleasure myself. You are not to move."

"Please, let me do it. I promise to make you feel so good."

She gave a low laugh. "Yes, I'm sure you will. But I want you to understand I control your orgasms. I control how I climax. If you are very good, and if you don't move, I may let you pleasure me."

His jaw clenched. He seemed to battle his lust for fulfillment against his usual routine of being in charge. His true nature won, and she caught all the signs of excitement shudder through his body at the thought of letting her lead. "Yes, Summer."

"Very nice."

She eased over the carved wooden footboard, a perfect prop for her thighs. Slowly, she spread her legs, her shaved pussy open to his gaze. "You've made me very wet, Rafe." Resting her fingers on the swollen lips, she coated her juices over her hardened clit. "I can only imagine how your hot, wet tongue would feel rubbing over my clit, thrusting inside." She pushed a finger in her slit and moaned. Her other hand worked her breast, rolling and pinching a tight nipple in rhythm with her finger. "Do you want to know how I feel?"

"Yes." His voice was ragged.

"Slick and hot and juicy. Oh, that feels so good, hmm, I need more." She added another finger and built up her speed, her knuckle rubbing over the nub pounding for release. She threw her head back on the bed and brought her knees up, spreading wider.

"Summer, please! Let me come to you."

"Not yet. I'm hot and tight, just begging for your cock and your fingers and your mouth to take me. Oh, I'm so close, I feel it, so good, ahh!" She came in a rush, her pussy clamping down on emptiness as shudders shook her. Knowing he watched every movement and saw all of her secrets intensified the pleasure. Spasms wracked her. She moaned in satisfaction then rose from the bed.

He knelt in perfect submission on the carpet. Sweat dripped from his brow and his skin gleamed to a high sheen He fought for control as his rock hard thighs trembled with exertion, and every muscle shuddered. Her heart soared at his ravaged features. Satisfaction pounded through her and lit her heart. *My God, he is perfect.* The masculine beauty of a man holding himself back, of submitting to such a deep need to release on her terms, was the most incredible gift. As if he were unable to speak coherently, a groan escaped.

She purred and stroked his damp hair, pushing the curls away from his brow. "Poor baby, you've been so good. I think you need a present. Tell me what you would like."

He struggled for words, to put his fantasy into reality. Asking for what he wanted was a big step in the path of submission. "I want to lick your pussy."

"Yes, baby, I think you deserve that. I'd like to come again. Stay exactly where you are. You are not to rub your cock against anything while you pleasure me. You are not allowed to come; do you understand?"

"Yes, Summer." She positioned herself on the floor in front of him, propping one spiked heel on each of his shoulders. She opened her legs wide and spread out before him like a present.

"Oh, God, you're so beautiful."

"Show me how much you want me."

He bent his head. Her hips arched at the first lick over her wet slit. His hot mouth opened slow and easy, stroking her swollen folds, teasing her clit, giving her just a tiny taste of what she really needed. She rolled her head back and forth and pushed her pussy higher. "More, give me more." He obediently plunged his tongue into her dripping heat. Over and over, he thrust, using his finger to rotate and massage her clit. The edge hovered in front of her, blurry and beckoning. She neared the peak and cried out, "Now, make me come now!"

He sucked on her clit and sank his fingers deep inside. She screamed as the orgasm ripped through her, shredding her with sheer pleasure. He gave a hoarse shout and milked her climax to the last shudder, then lapped up her juices and pressed kisses to her trembling thighs.

She practically purred in satisfaction at the deep-seated orgasm. "Very nice." Slowly, she rose to her feet. "I'm going to pour myself a glass of wine, baby. Would you like something?"

His face reflected raw anger and naked need. He growled low in his throat, shaking with need. "Are you kidding me? What the hell game do you think you're playing?"

Her voice slapped like a whip. "What did you just say to me?"

He jerked back but gritted his teeth in determination. "I'm dying here. I need to come."

"Oh, you need to come, do you?" She walked over and lifted his chin, towering over him. "You'll come when I tell you to."

"I can't last any longer." The agony of holding back his orgasm etched his face. "Please, Summer."

She softened. "I know it hurts, baby. But if you hang on, I promise you the best orgasm you ever had in your life. Do you trust me?"

"What?"

She cupped his face and gazed into his eyes. Their soulful depths pulled her in. *Dear God, when he leaves, he'll take a part of me. Could I have fallen in love after only a few hours?* "Do you trust me? Do you trust me to take you to the extremes of pleasure and keep you safe?"

"Yes."

His admission tore through her. She pressed a kiss to his lips, sliding her tongue over his carved mouth and dipping inside for a quick taste. "Thank you. Stay here a moment." She walked over to the bedroom bureau, slid out a drawer, and came back with a large black ring and lube. "Stand, please."

He rose to his feet. His erection pulsed in demand, but she concentrated on lubing up the ring, and then rubbed the liquid on his cock. Slowly, she slid the ring up his length to the base, worked it over his testicles, and tested the position. He twitched in agony and shook his head. "What the hell is this? Oh, God, I can't take it."

"Yes, you can. It's a cock ring. It will help you control your orgasm until I'm ready. The ring restrains your testicles so when you come, it will be much more intense. Unless you want to use your safe word?"

A flicker of temptation lit his eyes. Just as quickly, his head bowed in submission. His dark desires needed to be filled, and he understood she'd give him what he sought. "No, Summer."

"Very good. Resume kneeling and I will bring us some wine and snacks."

She left the bedroom.

Chapter Five

*R*AFE STARED AT THE WOMAN in front of him and wondered if he was in heaven or hell. Felt like both. His body didn't belong to him any longer—every inch of skin and muscle belonged to her. Usually so sharp about the next maneuver to make a woman experience pleasure, instead his mind fogged. Every reaction was completely tied to her words, her commands, her praise. In a matter of one evening, all his military training and dominant mannerisms faded away under the sting of her voice or the sharp bite of her spiked heel.

What the hell happened to him? A pounding cadence enveloped his dick and wrecked his concentration. The cock ring tamped down the urgent need to spill his seed, but his swollen flesh ached with the need for release. The strange line of pain and pleasure caused him more arousal than ever imagined. He'd never wanted to come so badly in his life. Even worse, he'd do anything she commanded if she gave him release.   By giving his trust, he bound this woman to take care of his needs. So far, he'd never experienced such soul-wracking pleasure by giving a woman an orgasm orally. Sure, he loved getting a woman off, but she took it to a whole new level. Her spicy taste drugged him, her slick heat clenching around his tongue in a fury that stripped away his barriers and any neat control he imagined he owned.

The cock ring kept him uncomfortably hard, but excitement slithered underneath the surface of his pain. A raw lust he needed to unearth. And the only way was through Summer's commands.

"Tell me about your brothers," she said. Her fingers stroked his hair and caressed the line of his jaw. Her soothing touch gentled the lunging beast of want threatening to overtake him.

"They're all dealers like me. Rick is the oldest and he came out to Vegas first. Then he convinced Rome to join him. Remington is still in Atlantic City. When I got out of the military, I stayed in AC for a while, but I felt like I needed a chance. Felt like home was suddenly closing in on me. So, I decided to move to Vegas and join Rick and Rome."

"I love that your Mom named all of you with the letter R. Must've caused some humorous situations."

Rafe grinned. "Yeah, let's just say Pop ended up pointing his finger and saying 'you.' Mom is a bit OCD and liked the organized structure of the names. I think it's embarrassing as hell. Kinda like wearing the same clothes as triplets."

"Are any of your brothers married?"

"No. But Rick and Rome are now both hooked up with serious relationships. I see marriage in their future. Met them through FANTA-C. That's how I found out about the agency and got a referral."

She paused in feeding him a cracker smeared with brie. "What? They both met their wives through FANTA-C?"

He chuckled at the look of surprise on her face. "Yep. Better watch out, baby, seems the agency is magic when it comes to the Steele brothers."

She smiled at him. The luminous light in her blue eyes squeezed his heart with longing. God, she was beautiful. Her angelic face expressed a pure openness he rarely glimpsed in a woman. She mirrored the perfect twist of naughty and nice that would make a man happy every morning he woke up in her bed. "I'm not afraid of commitment," she said, softly. "I'm tired of hiding who I am. I want a man to be my partner and friend in life. In public. And I want a man strong enough to submit in the bedroom."

Her words shook him like an answering thunderstorm. What if she offered him the opportunity to be with her past one night? He pushed the tempting thought aside. "Maybe you don't have as much to lose," he blurted. As his cock pulsed, he waited for the sting of punishment from his outburst, but she stared back, her face serious.

"I teach third grade," she said softly. "I'm in the PTA, afterschool clubs, and tutor privately. I have a nice little house with a white picket fence and roses in the backyard. My best friends are married for years with babies and vanilla lifestyles. I don't want to give any of that up, and I don't intend to. But I need to be who I am, and if that consists of joining a private BDSM club, or finding a partner who isn't afraid of experimentation, I'm going to follow it." She paused and pressed her thumb against his lips. "What are you so afraid of? That your brothers would never forgive you? That you would be called less than a man? Or that you'll finally find what you've been looking for?"

He imagined Summer by his side, in public and private. Building a life. Free of restrictions, completely submitting to her every demand. To finally feel the freedom of pleasure on his own terms.

His cock throbbed and his heart wept.

The idea of his brothers staring in wide-eyed shock and horror flashed in his mind. Shame pulsed with the knowledge that a well-known sergeant fell to his knees before a woman in leather, enjoying the sting of a slap in punishment. No. How could he be like this? Perhaps when he finally claimed her, finally climaxed, he'd experience a satisfying relief and could walk away.

A fleeting glimpse of recognition flickered in her eyes, as if she suspected his secret thoughts. She stepped back and put away the wine and snacks, then came back into the room with determination. "I seem to be craving your touch on my body," she snapped. "You will leave your cock ring on. Stand."

He rose, his knees sore from kneeling in the same position, even with the thick carpet. *Dear God, if I touch her for too long I'll explode—with or without the damn ring.* He dug deep and clawed for the control he'd need to make love to her without coming. She lay down on the bed, her gorgeous white blonde hair spread over the burgundy satin pillows. Then spread her legs. His mouth watered. Her breasts and nipples reminded him of cherries on whipped cream. Her abandon ratcheted his own desire, her pussy naked and open, ready for him to serve.

He settled on the bed, pressing on top of her. Licking and biting the sensitive curve of her neck, he plumped her breasts, drew a nipple into his mouth, and sucked hard. She arched and he relished the quick flip of control. He feasted on her breasts, her belly, and then dove between her thighs. Sucking and tonguing her to a sharp orgasm, he helped her ride out the spasms, greedy for more. The need to thrust into her tight heat gripped him in a frenzy.

"Please, Summer, please."

"Tell me what you want." Her eyes glazed. "Tell me exactly."

"I want to fuck you. Let me fuck you."

She smiled and licked her lips. "Yes, Rafe, you may fuck me." The relief of freedom surged, victory finally close. She grabbed a condom from the table, ripped off the wrapper, and held it above him. "Remove the ring."

He stripped the restriction from his cock. Blood surged through him and he gasped as he fought to hang on.

"Good." She covered him in seconds, then flipped over and knelt on all fours. He almost exploded at the sight of her perfect ass held high in the air. Grasping her hips, he positioned her, and then drove to the hilt in her heat.

Sparks shimmered behind his eyes at the sharp pierce of pleasure. Her pussy clenched on his cock like hungry, greedy fingers, her juices dripping around him. He cried out in ecstasy.

"You are not allowed to come."

Her words shattered his sensual fog. "What? No, I can't, please—"

"No coming. Now fuck me."

He moved, plunging in and out. His control slipped away with each thrust, the slow, steady rhythm ripping away his sanity and leaving a raw, bleeding need to be filled by her. Tears pricked the back of his lids. Her pussy clenched around him.

"Tell me what you want! Now."

A sob caught in his throat. "I want to come, Summer. Fuck! Let me come inside you!"

"Very nice, baby. Come with me, now!"

He gave a guttural cry of victory and dove deep, his balls slapping against her ass. "Ah!" He shot hot cum, the orgasm gripping every muscle and hurled him over the edge. His toes curled into the mattress as he pumped furiously and released every last drop. The climax shimmered for what felt like endless minutes, going on and on, until he collapsed on the bed, completely spent. She whispered his name and cuddled into him, stroking his back and kissing his cheek. He floated in a strange space of complete peace and bliss he'd never known existed in this life plane. Stray tears clung to his cheeks but she licked them away, and he was too far-gone to care.

Emotionally and physically wrecked, fucked out of his mind, he closed his eyes and surrendered to the nothingness.

Chapter Six

SUMMER GLANCED AT THE clock by the bureau. Six AM. Dawn had broken beyond the bat cave blinds of the bedroom suite. He slept with a peaceful slumber that broke her heart. They'd woken up a few more times to make love and snuggle, but it had taken him a while to surface after diving into the sub space after his first orgasm.

She took in his strong, muscled body, carved chest, olive skin. Dark curls tumbled over his forehead and her fingers itched to touch them. A rough five o'clock shadow stubbled his chin with a rough sexiness she craved on a full time basis. *Oh yeah, I'm completely screwed. And not in a good way.*

She'd fallen hard for Rafe Steele.

Dear God, how can I ever go back to my old life? He'd wrecked her for all others—wrecked her for the normal vanilla sex with its nice boundaries and neat actions that barely scratched the surface of deep emotion. By giving in to his needs, his want, he'd given her a priceless gift.

She sat up in bed. What had she done? How had he snuck past her defenses so quickly? When she'd visited that club for her orientation, she met many subs and not one had connected with her. Her experimentation with play called to her soul, but he'd ruined her for every man who might follow. Unless she asked him to stay.

As if reading her mind, he opened his eyes.

His smile lit up her insides with a glowing warmth. She wanted the time to treasure him, to show him the exotic world of submission that completed both of their souls. But he needed to have the courage to try to reach out for what he wanted.

He needed to take the dare.

He pulled her down for a kiss. His lips moved over hers with the knowledge of a lover, and she gave it all back to him before finally pulling away. "What's wrong?" His voice was gritty and rough from sleep.

"It's morning," she said simply.

Recognition dawned. He sat up, the sheets twisted around his hips. A mix of trepidation and want filled his eyes. "Are you kicking me out of the bed?" He tried for humor, but it fell flat in the waiting silence.

She took a deep breath. She expected honesty from a sub, but that honesty began with her. "No. But are you ready to hear what I really want?"

He squeezed his eyes shut, as if preparing himself. "Yes."

"I want you." The words hung in the room like smoke after a gunfire. "I never expected to feel like this, but I want to see you again. I'd like to see where this relationship can go, if you're willing to try. You're an incredible man, Rafe Steele. You have everything I've always wanted, and after one night, I don't want to let you go. But if you don't feel the same way about me, I release you. Our contract ended at dawn. I will thank you for the most incredible evening of my life, and move on. I will never contact you again, and everything that happened behind these doors will never be mentioned."

Raw emotion glimmered in his eyes. His jaw clenched. Unclenched. Then the words spilled out of his mouth. "I don't want to let you go. I've never felt like this before. But I don't know if I can commit to this lifestyle."

"I dare you."

He sucked in his breath. "Dare me to what?"

"To be honest with what you want. I'm not asking you to admit the lifestyle to your brothers or in public. This is private, between us. But I need to know you'll explore it with me. And give me everything I ask behind closed doors."

He seemed to struggle between the lure of his fantasy and the fear of reality. Her heart pounded and the blood squeezed through her veins. He needed to make his own choice or they could never work.

"I can't do it yet, Summer. I'm not ready."

She acknowledged his limitation and a heavy grief pressed into her limbs. Perhaps he would never be ready, but she needed to move down her own path and find her own answers. Tears pricked her eyelids. She leaned forward, kissed him, and slid out of bed.

"I understand, I really do. But I can't follow you right now. Thank you for everything you gave me, I won't forget it." She paused. "I won't forget you."

She gathered her clothes and closed the bedroom door behind her.

***

Rafe listened to the door shut and sat in the silence of the room.

She'd left.

An ache spread from his gut slowly outward, until his body throbbed as if he'd contracted the flu. Why was he having such a hard time letting her go? They'd had sex. Great sex, but it had only been one night. Relationships didn't form that fast, right?

He'd finally surrendered to his fantasy and it was everything he'd always dreamed. But now it was time to get back to reality. He'd find a woman to play lightly with, but no one who wanted a hardcore sub in the bedroom. Fantasies weren't meant to be forever.

Still, the idea Summer would find another sub to torture, fuck, heal, and pleasure made him sick. Rafe forced the images out of his head and tried to be rational. She led a different life from him and he couldn't follow. No way would he go to some club and be outed. No way would he take a backseat in a relationship when he was used to commanding on a daily basis. He'd just wanted a taste for the bedroom.

Now, it was over.

He clenched his jaw and climbed out of bed. Time to return to his real life, a life that was big and wonderful. He adored his brothers, his job, and his new home. Now, that he'd gotten his fantasy out of his system, Rafe was sure he'd be more satisfied finding a woman who was better suited to him.

He vowed to put Summer Preston out of his mind forever.

Chapter Seven

*T*WO WEEKS LATER, Rafe cursed his weakness and waited at the curb in front of Lakeside Elementary school. He watched kids file out of the school, clutching parents' hands and chattering excitedly about the day. A pang of longing cut deep.

He had better make a move or they'd think he was some kind of weird stalker, which he was, but only when it came to one hot Dominatrix teacher who spun his world like a tornado and refused to leave him in peace.

He tamped down a sigh and made his way to the front door, stopping at the sign-in desk. "I'm here to see Summer Preston," he said.

The gray haired lady peered over her glasses with suspicion. "Is she expecting you?"

"No." He took out his military ID and flashed it. "But she's a friend."

The woman's face softened when she caught that he'd served, and she nodded. "Fill this out. I'll ring her and let her know. Classroom 18."

"Thanks." He filled out the form and walked down the hall. Brightly colored pictures filled the painted blue walls, along with essays stapled to construction paper and various science projects. Children rushed past him in giggling groups, amidst teachers with clipboards trying to herd them into neat lines for dismissal. Rafe hid a smile, experiencing a sense of déjà vu from his own school days, and found room 18.

He went in.

She sat behind a large desk, back towards him, speaking with a dark-haired girl with thick black glasses. He waited quietly while her soft voice drifted to his ears, soothing him immediately.

"Hannah, this is the third day you haven't turned in homework. I told you we'd work together on the math problems. Is there something you don't understand?"

The little girl was silent. She ducked her head, dragged her foot, and blinked those big dark eyes until Rafe figured he'd be putty in her small hands. "No."

"No, you don't understand the math homework? Or no, you don't need any help?"

"I don't need any help."

"Is there another reason you're not doing the assignment? Are mom and dad okay?"

Hannah straightened up in sheer panic. "No!" she burst out. "I'll—I'll do the homework. I just...forgot."

Summer studied her for a while, and then slowly nodded. "I gave you two sheets for tonight. I also wrote a note to your mom. It's in your folder to bring home."

The little girl's lower lip trembled a bit. Rafe frowned. Something was going on. Seemed Summer caught the same vibe, because she squeezed

Hannah's hand in support. "You can talk to me if something's bothering you, honey. We can figure it out together."

Hannah stayed silent.

Summer sighed and tucked her folder into her backpack. "Better get going before you miss the bus."

The little girl grabbed the backpack and tore out of the classroom, racing right by him without a second look.

Summer spun halfway around in her chair and rubbed her temples. Rafe took a moment to drink in her presence. Her silvery hair was clipped back in a loose knot and she had glasses like Hannah's perched on her nose. She wore a black pencil skirt, white blouse, and flat ballet type shoes. The proper, conservative vibe she gave off was ridiculously hot. He imagined her with a ruler in hand while she disciplined him mercilessly, and his dick got so hard, he cleared his throat, hoping no other children suddenly darted in.

She gasped and turned. Their gazes met and locked, and the simmering sexual tension exploded around them. Rafe caught his breath at the punch of pure heat. God, what was it about this woman? He'd been hoping if he saw her again, he'd convince himself it was just a lingering memory he wanted to hold on to. His original plan was to see her again, exchange a few words, and convince himself it had only been the exoticness of that one night bonding them together.

Instead, he was in the classroom of an elementary school and craved to drag her onto the desk and fuck her like an animal.

"What are you doing here?" Her voice came out a bit ragged. Was that a glint of hope in her blue eyes or his imagination? Had she been thinking about him, too?

He walked in and shut the door behind him.

"I'm sorry to bother you at work. I just—I just needed to see you."

Summer stood up, her arms clasped in front of her chest. "Is something wrong?"

"Yes."

"What?"

"I can't stop thinking about you."

His words were raw and honest. He had nowhere left to hide, but he wasn't ready to take a full on leap. Rafe needed more time with her to figure it all out. He'd finally decided one night wasn't enough to slake his desires, so he had another proposition to bring her. If she'd take it.

Feeling vulnerable, he waited, but a smile curved her lips and she took a step forward. "I can't stop thinking about you either."

Relief cut through him. "What are we going to do about it?"

"What do you want to do about it?"

They circled each other. Her scent rose to his nostrils—a spicy, musk that defined the bad girl underneath all that surface civility. She was completely intoxicating, and he tightened his fists to keep from dragging her to him to steal a kiss. She wouldn't like that, though. Would probably punish him.

The thought should piss him off and remind him he wasn't a true sub.

Instead, the idea of her dominating him again made his cock twitch in need.

This time, her smile came slow and sexy, with the wicked knowledge she turned him on. Why did he want to drop to his knees and serve?

"I have a proposal," he finally said.

She inclined her head. "Go ahead."

"One night wasn't enough. Not for me. But I'm not ready to commit to be a full-time sub. I'm looking for more time. Time to see if we're good together for more than one night of great sex."

She took a long while before answering. Rafe appreciated her quietness, the way she didn't jump into emotion and chatter nonstop. Summer seemed to sift through his words, analyzing, thinking, before she answered. Another quality he adored in a woman and rarely found. "I didn't think this was something you wanted," she said quietly.

"I didn't think so either. Until I spent the night with you."

"This is new to me, too, Rafe. After the time we spent together, I realized I was more fulfilled than I'd ever been, but I'm learning my way. We can learn it together."

His heart pounded. Was he seriously going through with this? A relationship where he was dominated in the bedroom? He could still walk away and go back to his old life. Problem was, his old life wasn't satisfying any longer. He'd tried dating since Summer, and each woman fell flat, until the emptiness inside his gut spread, and he longed to feel alive again. Maybe just a little more time with her could help him decide. Maybe bringing them out of the bedroom and into the world would give him balance.

"I can't give any promises. I don't know what will happen between us, but I crave you, Summer. I lay awake at night and think of your hands on my body; of fucking you long, and deep, and slow, and I explode. Will you spend Saturday with me? I have the day off. I'd love to spend some time with you."

Her joyous smile gave him fierce satisfaction. God, he got off on pleasing her. "I'd love that. I'm free Saturday."

"Good. I'll pick you up at ten am. Dress casual."

"Keds?"

He laughed. "Perfect. Put my number in your phone." They exchanged cell numbers. "See you Saturday. Oh, and Summer?"

"Yeah."

His eyes glittered with sensual demand. "Bring the catsuit."

Rafe didn't turn to see how his words affected her.

Chapter Eight

"**Y**OU'VE GOT TO BE KIDDING."

Summer looked up at the massive black horse that towered over her petite frame. She chewed on her thumbnail, considering if he'd eat her or just throw her off with a shake of his head.

Rafe grinned and patted her denim-clad rear. The light touch burned right through the fabric and tingled. "You'll be fine, sweetheart. Clyde is made for beginners, gentle as anything. Come on, I'll help you up."

Her head tilted all the way back with a touch of panic. "How? Gonna throw me in the air and hope I hit the saddle?"

Rafe shook his head and dragged over the step stool. She climbed up with shaky legs and he helped her slide onto the horse's back. Clutching the saddle horn, he adjusted her stirrups and showed her to hold the reins, firmly but with a light touch.

"Just remember, you're the boss. Treat him kindly, but if he gives you attitude, pull back on the reins so he knows who's in charge. Sound familiar?"

She glowered at him, but he threw back his head and laughed. "Very funny."

Summer watched with hungry eyes as he strode over to his own mount and climbed up on the saddle. The faded jeans cupped his rear like a gift, and the short- sleeved, button-down green shirt emphasized the golden glints in his dark eyes. Old, battered work boots clad his feet. He was mouth-watering and delicious, reminding her of those old Western movies where the men were crude, rude, and a bit dirty. She loved his hard edge, and the way he'd allowed himself to surrender to her that night.

"Follow me on the trail. Clyde knows the way. When we go downhill, lean back and kick your feet out a bit in the stirrups. When we go up, lean forward. Got it?"

"Can we go hiking instead?"

"You'll have fun. Promise."

He took off on a slow, leisurely gait and Summer held her breath for the first few minutes. But Clyde was steady, and soon she began to relax, enjoying the scenery around her. The majestic mountains towered and squeezed around her. Colors exploded in her sight, from the red rocks to the sweep of azure sky to the scattered green brush. The sound of the horses' hooves on the trail rose to her ears, and Summer breathed in the hot, dusty air, enjoying the burn of the sun on her face that she'd never complain about in Vegas.

"I'd never pictured you riding a horse," she called out, swaying side to side with Clyde. "Aren't you from Jersey?"

"I'm an animal lover. Pop took us horseback riding on vacation one year and I fell in love. I took a bunch of lessons. Think if I lived on a farm, I'd buy my own horse. I've been coming out here to Dusty's Ranch on a regular basis. Thought you'd appreciate it."

"Now that I'm over my terror, I kind of like it. It's peaceful."

"Something about being on a horse gets you out of your own head, you know? I feel more connected. Part of something bigger. Afraid I'm gonna break into song?"

She giggled and he turned around and gave her a wink. She liked this side to Rafe; he was fun and knew how to tease. Summer imagined him kicking back with his brothers, his face relaxed as they bantered back and forth. "You think you can scare me with that threat? I was the lead in my school play."

"What was it?"

"*Mama Mia.*"

"You win. I'm scared."

She stuck out her tongue, but his chuckle said he'd caught the gesture.

They rode through rocky trails and hills at a leisurely pace, a comfortable silence surrounding them. "How long have you been a teacher?" he asked curiously.

"Four years."

"Do you wish you had studied a different career? You said your parents pushed you into teaching."

Summer tilted her head, considering. "I was interested in a lot, especially the fine arts. Painting was a hobby of mine. I loved acting and dancing, which is how I got the lead in a lot of my school plays. But my parents wanted me to have security and a job that brought honor. Since I'm needle phobic, and can't stand law, it left teaching. Looking back, I don't regret that decision. I like helping my students, and making a difference. I like who I am when I'm teaching."

"You seemed very good with that little girl. Hannah? Did you ever find out why she wasn't doing her homework?"

Summer sighed. "Yes, her mom finally told me. Her dad is military and had to go on leave. Seems Hannah is going through separation anxiety."

Rafe's shoulders stiffened. After the heartbreaking story he'd shared with her, she bet he understood exactly what that family would be experiencing. "People forget it's not just the servicemen who suffer. Wives, siblings, children. It affects them all."

"What about you, Rafe? Do you regret enlisting after what happened?"

The horses came to an open dry field and Rafe brought them to a stop. Tugging on the reigns, he turned the horse around and faced her. The jolt of his inky eyes meeting hers made her heart pause, then gallop like a thoroughbred. "No. I learned early on each piece of our lives connects to another. Somehow, even with the shit, I believe it all happened for a reason. I hated losing Ben. Hated how getting that stupid medal made me feel. But I also know in the big picture, I'd end up doing it all over again because that's how it has to be."

Summer stared at his beautiful face. He was so much more than she'd ever expected. A brave, kind man who'd been bent but not broken. A man who believed in faith and a higher purpose. The kind of man she wanted in her life.

Her throat tightened and she smiled. "I'm glad, too. Because now you're here with me."

A startled look crossed his features. Then he smiled back, and Summer wondered if you could fall in love with someone in a moment.

***

"My ass hurts."

Rafe slid his gaze over her gorgeous, lush rear currently placed on the picnic bench. He'd tried to tempt her to a five-star dinner with wine and French cuisine. She'd spotted a taco food truck and begged him to stop, and now they feasted on the best frikkin tacos he'd ever had, accompanied by slaw, rice, beans, and washed down with Coca Cola.

Pure heaven.

"I can help you with that problem," he offered. "A good rubdown at my place?"

"Is that a proposition?" she teased.

"I'd rather term it a seduction. So much more pleasurable for both of us."

"Perhaps." Her gaze raked over his figure. "Perhaps having you chained and naked at my feet would be my preferred form of seduction." Suddenly, her innocent, good-girl persona drifted away and he was faced with a woman who knew exactly what she wanted and how to get it. Sex practically oozed from her pores. Demand glinted from her blue eyes. His cock hardened, and breath strangled his lungs. Rafe fought the urge to bow his head in front of her, drop to his knees, and offer his body for her use.

"That could work, too," he managed.

Her slow smile promised heaven and a bit of hell. "Would you like to come back to my place and play with me?"

He knew what the invitation meant. Rafe would be under her direction. Her rules. The thought of another evening like they'd experienced caused the blood to rush to both heads so fast the world tilted.

"Yes."

"Finish your tacos. Then we'll go."

"Yes, Summer."

Her pleased nod wracked him with anticipation. They quickly finished and drove to her house, a pretty, white- trimmed cape cod on a tree-lined street. It was exactly as he'd pictured her house. Small, neat, and simple, with a front porch, postage stamp lawn, and the bright spill of flowers hanging from various hooks.

Inside, it was more of the same. A cheery yellow kitchen with stainless steel appliances led to the right, and the left was a powder blue living room with comfortable white furniture, patterned throw pillows, and bookcases overflowing with books. The place smelled like coconut. Braided rugs tossed on hardwood floors gave the impression of a beachy cottage filled with warmth.

"I love your place," he commented.

She grabbed two bottles of water from the refrigerator and walked to his side. "Thanks. I don't need much but I love the privacy of a house rather than a condo."

"Yeah, I can see why. I love my condo for convenience but being smashed between neighbors and a constant flow of traffic gets old. I was thinking about upgrading to a house."

Summer handed him a bottle of water. He took a sip. "I like the idea of making you scream without anyone around to hear."

And just like that, they flicked the switch.

He stilled. Looked at her. Dressed in jeans, Keds, and a yellow cotton shirt, she shouldn't look dangerous. But she did. She looked like she could feast on him whole, and his body trembled in response.

"Do you remember your safe word, Rafe?" she drawled.

"Blackjack."

"Very good. Now, would you like me to change into a more appropriate outfit?"

He swallowed. Rafe doubted he could wait that long. He ached to have her naked and available as quickly as possible. "No. I think you're perfect just as you are."

She considered his answer, then nodded. "Thank you. But from now on when I ask you a question, you will say, 'Whatever pleases you, Summer.'"

"Okay."

"Say it."

He stiffened. Why was his heart beating so fast? She wasn't dressed in leather and stilettos? Yet, he realized now it didn't matter. It was like slipping on a cloak, she shimmered with demand and arrogance. She was a true Mistress.

His Mistress.

"Whatever pleases you, Summer."

"Very nice." Her voice poured over him like warm, sticky honey. "I'd like you to go into my bedroom. First door on the right at the top of the stairs. Take off all your clothes. Then kneel in front of the bed and wait for me."

Arousal twisted his belly. The command was clear, but still he hesitated, caught between wanting to obey and knowing in his head it was crazy to take orders from a woman. Why did he like it so much? Why wasn't he more like his brothers?

Her voice struck like a Scorpion's sting. "Have you decided to safe word?"

"No."

"Then I suggest you obey my order before you earn a punishment."

The threat only got him more turned on. "Summer, I don't think— "

"That's the problem. Your job is not to think. Your job is to do what I say, when I say it. I'll give you one last time to obey. Go upstairs, take off your clothes, and kneel."

Rafe dragged in a breath and let his body win the war. Need burned deep within him. If he walked away without touching her, fucking her, claiming her, he'd shatter.

Rafe went upstairs. Her bedroom was a soothing green like the spill of an Irish meadow. He took off his clothes and laid them on the back of a white rocker. Squeezing his eyes shut, he knelt on the rug in front of the door and waited.

He heard the creak of floorboards. The uneven harshness of his breathing. The hum of the air conditioner. Time slowly ticked by, and anticipation cranked up notch-by-notch, until his skin tingled and every sound pricked at his ears.

Finally, he caught her scent.

Rafe's eyes opened.

He ached to look at her, but instinct veered his gaze downward. She walked slowly around him, her fingers tousling his hair, sliding across his shoulders. "Beautiful," she murmured. Her nails raked down his spine and he fought a shiver. "You are like every sexual fantasy come to life for me, Rafe Steele. I want to do some very wicked things to you. I want to make you come so hard you won't have another rational thought for hours. Would you like that?"

"Yes, Summer." His voice felt like a croak, but she kept touching him, and it felt so fucking good.

"Rise, please."

He stood up. She was inches shorter than him without her boots, but her command of his space was total. She brought his chin up, forcing him to look at her. "Kiss me."

With a groan, he lowered his head and took her mouth. Tongue thrusting deep into the silky, wet cave, he plundered and drank her sweet taste until his hands fisted at his sides in desperate need to touch her. But he held back, knowing she hadn't given him permission yet.

Summer took everything he gave, kissing him back with wild abandon. When she broke the kiss, her lips were swollen and her blue eyes glassy with lust. His cock surged and he leaned in, ready to grab and take what he wanted, but managed to battle back the impulse and stay still.

"Very nice," she purred. "You're learning, baby. Undress me."

He divested her of clothes with quick, economical movements, not wanting to be teased anymore. She allowed him full reign, until she stood naked, her bare pussy lips gleaming with moisture. Hard, red nipples poking at him in demand.

"May I touch you, Summer?"

"Yes. Touch and suck my breasts."

He stroked her beautiful curves, his thumb tweaking her nipples, playing with the peaks until they were so sensitive, she shuddered each time he grazed one. Pinching a bit harder, he finally lowered his head and sucked on her nipples. Biting, licking, nibbling, he spent long, long minutes pleasuring her breasts, until her fingers tangled in his hair and dragged him away.

Her skin gleamed with wetness. Her breath came in tiny pants. Satisfaction cut through him, loving how he was able to affect her.

"Please give me more, Summer," he begged. "Let me lick your pussy."

She stepped away, control seeping back to her voice. "Not yet. Lie on the bed, please. Hands over your head. Feet spread apart."

Rafe wanted to argue, but excitement flared in his gut, pushing him to obey. When he was positioned on the bed, he heard a drawer open, then the clink of metal. "I'm going to handcuff you to the bed, Rafe. These are safety cuffs and can be pulled apart, but if you panic, use your safe word. Tell me what it is again."

"Blackjack."

"Say it and I'll stop immediately. Are you okay?"

"Yes, Summer."

"Very good." She fastened the cuff and attached them to the bedpost, checking the fit. "Are these too tight?"

"No, Summer."

She did the other hand and then knelt on the bed in between his spread knees. His dick was so hard; it throbbed for the wet heat of her mouth.

"You are so gorgeous, spread-eagled for me, ready for me to pleasure you," she said. "Tell me what you want me to do to you."

His breath shuddered in his chest. "Whatever pleases you, Summer."

"You deserve a reward for that. I'm going to suck your cock now. You are not allowed to come."

And then she lowered her mouth and took him fully inside.

Rafe groaned. Pulled at the cuffs as the sharp waves of pleasure cut through him. God, her mouth was so hot, wet, and tight. She didn't bother teasing him or with foreplay, no, this was about pushing him straight to the edge, as her tongue swirled the tip, dragged down the underside, and her throat opened to took his full length. He fucked her mouth, writhing on the bed as the climax came hurtling at him, poised on the edge.

"I'm gonna come!"

She scraped the edge of her teeth over his cock and stars exploded in his eyes. "Don't come, baby. Not till I say."

He gritted his teeth and held on. By the time she released him, sweat beaded his skin, and his vision fogged with need. A wicked, satisfied laugh escaped her lips, and she shimmied up her body, straddling his face, her pussy open and waiting for him.

"Suck my pussy, Rafe."

"Oh, God, yes."

Her taste was pure heaven. Spicy and musky, he lapped at her labia, circling her hard clit with the tip of his tongue but no more. He teased her mercilessly, until her hips rotated and she was fucking his face, asking for more, and Rafe gave it to her, plunging his tongue into her pussy, working his lips against her swollen lips, over and over.

Her sweet cries and the desperate way she ground against him told him she was at the edge, and Rafe went crazy with the need to make her come all over him. He grasped her clit between his teeth, teasing both sides, then sucked hard.

Summer exploded. With a groan of satisfaction, he took it all, shuddering on the brink of his own orgasm, until her shuddering body finally withdrew and she collapsed on top of him.

He pulled at the handcuffs, frantic to throw her on her back and fuck her senseless, but the restraints made his arousal climb higher.

"Please, Summer," he groaned. "Please fuck me."

"Yes, baby, yes. You've been so good." She quickly fit him with a condom, climbed on top of his body, and sunk him deep into her channel. "Take me. Take it all."

She rode him fast and hard, like a wild mare on a stallion, taking more of her pleasure with no apology. Rafe bucked underneath, sinking deeper into her tight channel, her arousal soaking his dick as they fell into animal-like mating with bites and scratches and raw lust, fucking until his balls tightened up, and he came hard, spilling his seed into the condom while his body jerked frantically in violent pleasure.

The orgasm went on so long, Rafe felt like it was two for one, and he wondered if it was possible to die from such an agonizing and complete release.

Time blurred. She uncuffed him, laying on top of his chest, her wild hair spilling across his cheek. They rested. Breathed together.

Darkness fell around them, bringing sleep and a deep-seated peace Rafe had never experienced before.

He slept.

Chapter Nine

SUMMER FINISHED HELPING the kids pack up for the day, once again noticing Hannah separated herself from the group. Her heart ached for the little girl. She'd spoken to her mother about support for military families, but Summer also realized Hannah was a sensitive soul, and it may take her a while to sort out her emotions.

The kids filed out for the bus, and Hannah slowly loaded up her Hello Kitty pencil case into her backpack. A gentle knock on the door turned her head.

"Hello, Ms. Preston."

She pursed her lips at his very proper address, wondering if she should trade in her catsuit for her classic teacher outfit. Yeah, seems her sub needed a very proper spanking for his brattiness. God, she loved it.

Yet....

Their relationship was still a secret. He hadn't introduced her to his brothers, and liked to keep their interactions separate from his *real* life. At first, she'd understood, knowing they were exploring the sub/dom dynamics, and wasn't sure if they'd be able to take the relationship further than a few play sessions.

Over the past weeks, though, Summer had fallen in love with him. She sensed he felt the same, but held back, even during some of their intense sessions. Summer had brought up maybe visiting a club together and making some friends in the BDSM community. He'd quickly squashed the idea, saying he wanted them to keep it private. Rafe was still terrified of having his brothers find out. He kept her in a locked, dark corner to play and satisfy his sexual needs, but Summer didn't want the same type of relationships she'd had in the past.

She wanted to be with Rafe in a public relationship. Wanted to meet his family and his friends. Wanted to explore similar type people in her community.

Summer wanted it all.

Unfortunately, she didn't think Rafe wanted the same things.

Pushing back her heartache, she motioned him in. "Mr. Steele," she greeted back. "What a surprise. Have you come for our tutoring session?"

He cocked his hip out and regarded her. She loved the way he dominated in the daytime, and how deeply he surrendered for her at night. "Depends. If I get an A on the test, do I get a reward?"

A little voice chirped up. "Ms. Preston says the best reward for doing good in school is knowledge." Hannah frowned behind her glasses. "Knowledge is power. You shouldn't need lollipops to learn."

Summer pressed her lips together to keep from laughing. "Hannah is right, Mr. Steele," she scolded. "Perhaps you need another lesson to remind you?"

He cut her an amused look, then walked in. "Your name is Hannah right?" The little girl nodded. "My name is Rafe. I'm a friend of your teacher's."

"Nice to meet you." She slipped on her backpack. "I'm ready to go, Ms. Preston."

"See you tomorrow, Hannah."

The little girl stopped by the doorway. Rafe lowered to his knees so they were face to face. "You know; I was in the military for a number of years."

Summer sucked in a breath. What was he doing? She jumped up from her desk. "Umm, Hannah, you better go and— "

"My daddy's in the military," she said seriously. "Did you go away?"

Rafe nodded, never taking his gaze from her face. "Yes, I was in Afghanistan. Have you heard of it?"

She nodded. "Daddy's there. He'll be there for a whole year. I'm not going to see him."

"Yeah, that's really tough. I missed my brothers and my parents a lot when I was in Afghanistan. But you know what really helped me?"

"What?"

"I'd think about them doing really good at their jobs, and having fun, and being happy, and it made me happy. If I thought they were sad, or doing bad at work, that would've made me really sad."

Hannah ducked her head. "But I don't want to have fun when Daddy's away. That would be bad."

Rafe shook his head. "No, Hannah, it's not bad. It's exactly what your Dad wants. When he calls or Skypes with you, or visits on holidays, he wants to know you're having fun, and trying really hard in school, and playing with your friends and stuff. He doesn't want you to worry about him or be too sad. Sure, you're going to miss him. But knowing you're enjoying your life at home, taking care of your mom and your siblings, that helps him a lot. Does that make sense?"

Slowly, Hannah nodded. "I guess. You think my Daddy will come home okay like you?"

"Yes. I do. He has many great teammates making sure he's going home to you and your Mom. Your job is to help him not worry when he's over there. Have you been doing your homework and stuff? Playing with your friends? Talking to your mom about how you feel?"

"No. I've been too sad."

"I understand. But if you try to do those things, it will be better for everyone. Okay? Ms. Preston wants to tell your mom you're doing great in school. That will make everyone happy. Will you try?"

Summer pressed her hand to her mouth, waiting. The little girl seemed to consider his words seriously. "Yes. I'll try."

"Thank you, sweetheart." He smiled at her and unfolded his legs to full height. "Now, you better run for your bus."

"Bye!"

She disappeared. Rafe shut the door behind him and headed toward her desk. "I'm sorry if I was out of line. I just wanted to try and reach out and—what the— "

Summer flew into his arms. Pulling his head down, she kissed him, not able to express how deeply she felt for him. For his beautiful heart, and his generosity, and his kindness. For everything, he gave her, inside and outside the bedroom. For being the man she loved.

He kissed her back as fiercely. When she finally broke away, he looked a bit dazed. "What was that for?"

"I love you."

Shock flickered over his face. Rafe took a jerky step back. "What did you say?"

Summer pushed her hair back and groaned. "I'm sorry. I shouldn't have said it like that. I should've given you warning. I love you. I've been feeling like this for a while now, and I know it's probably still too soon, but it's how I feel. I love you. That's it."

"That's it, huh?" Rafe grinned and shook his head. "Should've known even a love confession would come out like a Dominatrix."

"I'm sorry." Misery shook through her voice. This was so embarrassing. Why couldn't she be the type of woman to wait for the man to say it first? "Thank you for helping with Hannah. I got carried away."

He closed the distance between them and frowned. "You're welcome. You're not taking it back, are you?"

Her cheeks flushed. "No."

"Good. Cause I love you too."

She gasped. Then looked at him suspiciously. "Are you sure? This isn't just a pity response, is it?"

He laughed, grabbed her, and pressed a hard kiss on her lips. "I don't say I love you to a woman just because I feel bad," he growled. "I'm crazy about you, Summer. Been falling in love with you a while now."

Joy bloomed. Everything seemed to slide into place and she babbled with excitement. "I'm dying to meet your brothers! Maybe we can do a dinner together and I can meet Sloane and Tara? Oh, and I know you've been a bit wary about this but I found out a casual friend of mine is a Sub and goes to this fabulous club, Chains. It's very discreet. I thought maybe we could go for an orientation. See if it fits us?"

"Wait a minute." Rafe interrupted, concern flickering over his face. "I told you I don't do clubs. I never will. I'm not putting my reputation at risk."

"Oh. Well, maybe we can discuss? I know their confidentiality agreements are air-tight."

"No, Summer. That's not something I'll ever do." A strange distance emanated between them. "And why don't we wait a bit longer before meeting my brothers?"

The joy of finding out he loved her faded into a faint dread. What was going on? He loved her, but he still didn't want her involved in his life fully.

"Are you ashamed of me, Rafe?"

"Of course not! I just don't want details of our personal relationship to spill over and be discussed. My brothers wouldn't understand. I just want to keep things private until we feel like we're ready."

Coldness laced her tone. "Are you afraid they'll suspect I'm a Dominatrix just by having dinner with them? Our sex life is private; I'm not looking to push you on that issue. I just want to meet your family because they're important to you."

"I understand. I want them to meet you too, eventually. I need more time. They're used to dealing with submissives."

Her heart squeezed. "I have nothing to hide. Do you?"

His dark eyes shot anger. "Yeah, I do, Summer. Sorry if I'm not as open as you, but I already said I wasn't comfortable with certain things. I love you. Isn't that enough? Things are going well. There's no reason to rock the boat."

Her gut lurched. Oh, God, it was happening again. He may love her, but not every part. He still thought they'd play at this dom/sub thing a bit and go back to a normal type relationship. Rafe didn't want to accept this was her true self. She craved dominance in the bedroom, and it wouldn't go away. The longer they pretended they were something they weren't, the harder it would get when the truth finally revealed itself.

Summer wouldn't go through that again. It had been too long a journey to be happy with the woman she was.

As fast as the joy had hit, now a deep-seated ache settled around her heart. "Rafe, I don't think you understand," she said softly. "I'm never going to change. I want to be a part of a club and community. I want your brothers to know who I really am, and who we are together, as a couple. I don't want to hide anymore."

"I'm not asking you to hide. I'm asking you to keep our sex life private."

She shook her head. "No, you're not. You're hoping I'll change into a more normal woman you can bring home to your family. You want permission to hide who I am, and I will not give you that. Take me the way I am or not at all."

"You're twisting my words," Rafe said forcefully. "Let's talk about this later. We just said I love you, which means I completely accept you. Just because I don't like the idea of anyone knowing I get on my knees to you, doesn't mean we can't work this out."

Grief overtook her. Summer wrapped her arms around her body for warmth. "You're beautiful on your knees, Rafe," she said brokenly. "You humble me with your submission. You're the one with the real power, don't you know that? Not me. You give me a gift I want to honor and keep safe. I want to give you back as much as I can, but when you deny what we are in the bedroom, you deny who we are as a couple." She stepped back, the distance growing between them. "I don't want that for either of us. I've come too far to step back now."

HIs eyebrow shot up. "So, that's it? We go from loving each other to breaking up because you think it has to be all or nothing?"

"Yes," she said simply.

He shook with pent-up anger. His voice lashed like a whip. "If you can't give me more time, maybe you're right. We were doing fine. I don't know why you want to walk away from something this good, just because I need to take it slow."

"You never intended on committing to be a sub in this relationship, did you?"

His silence was his answer. She understood now. In a way, the past weeks together was a mission for Rafe to try to wring submission out of his system. He figured with enough time, it would get boring and he'd be able to go back to his normal type sex life. Maybe he thought she'd agree with him, and they'd change back to a nice, vanilla couple.

"I can't live like that anymore," she said. "I'm sorry. It's not going to work between us, after all."

"You once dared me to take a chance on this relationship," he said furiously. "Well, I'm asking you to do that now. Take a chance on me."

Summer blinked past tears. "I already have," she whispered.

The silence blistered with unspoken hurt and accusations. With pain. "If this is what you want, so be it," he said.

The door closing behind him was the last sound in the room.

Chapter Ten

*R*AFE WATCHED HIS BROTHERS tear into a plate of nachos and wash them down with a pair of matching Coors Lite. His stomach twisted with tension, but he'd made his decision. He needed to tell his brothers the truth—then get Summer Preston back into his life and in his bed.

Thirty days of pure hell. That's how long it had taken him to realize he'd made the biggest mistake of his life by walking away. She'd been right all along. He'd tried to compartmentalize and make them a normal couple. Whatever the hell normal was. Rafe figured with enough time, they'd get over their kink and he'd finally be able to bring their relationship into the light.

So stupid. So selfish. The whole time, she'd been open and honest about what she wanted. Instead, he'd been the one to lie, to both of them, and now he paid the price.

Because his world without Summer was empty. Lackluster. Like going from a black and white to

Technicolor, he couldn't lie to himself and anybody else anymore.

Something shattered within him that day. He'd pushed past the pain and got back into his old life, but everything changed. Dealing cards, sharing a meal with his brothers, and dating a bunch of pretty, nameless women left him cold. His soul gaped open with an empty wound and nothing seemed to fill it. When he'd looked up private BDSM clubs on the internet and wondered if she had a new sub, the sick anger nearly tore him apart. Fierce emotion coursed through him at the image of her sweet face hiding a tigress's soul. He belonged to her, and she to him. Their weeks together proved he loved submitting to her. He was happier on his knees and showing his devotion than he'd ever been trying to dominate or control a woman in the bedroom. He missed the peace he found in the simple act of obeying, the falling away of barriers and thoughts and memories that usually haunted him. He was truly himself, raw and vulnerable, and she made him feel more cherished and adored than any woman could.

Rafe decided his biggest barriers sat beside him in the cracked leather booth, chowing down on appetizers in ignorant bliss. His first step was key to getting Summer to forgive him. Rafe tipped back his beer bottle for one last swig and faced his brothers. "I need to tell you guys something. Something that's been bothering me for a long time."

They shared a look. Rick dropped the chip he held in his hand and leaned in. Rome nodded with encouragement. "Go ahead, bro. We're listening."

Their rock solid support surrounded him. He took a deep breath. "I'm a submissive."

Rick raised one blond brow. "Get out."

His stomach turned but he kept his chin high and met his brother's stare head on. "Nope. I've known this for a while now, but I turned chicken shit and refused to admit it. Remember when I told you about my night FANTA-C arranged?"

Rome looked puzzled. "Yeah. You said she was a pretty sub you tied to your bed, but you weren't going to see her again."

Rafe winced. "I lied. I was hooked up with a Dominatrix. Her name is Summer, and I fell hard. I didn't want to admit that I could be a real sub, so I've been dating her and refusing to tell anyone. I think I was hoping we'd either break up, or become a normal couple."

Rick rolled his eyes. "Define normal. That's asinine. Everyone has some kink and there's nothing wrong with it."

Rome shook his head. "Sloane would kick your ass if she heard you saying shit like that, bro. So, what happened between you two?"

"We fell in love. She asked to meet you guys and maybe go to a BDSM club to be introduced to others in the BDSM community. I told her no way. I was still embarrassed of what people would think if anyone found out. Imagine me on my knees? I couldn't deal."

"Yeah, Sloane would definitely kick your ass. Just because you like to submit to a Dom who cares about you, doesn't make you weak."

"Yeah, I know that now. It took me a while, but I don't want to deny who I am anymore. I need to do anything to get Summer back. And I will." He pointed a finger at Rick. "I don't need to take any of your shit about this." Then he glared at Rome. "From either of you. Got it?"

Rome studied him in a thoughtful silence and he inwardly squirmed. His brother wiped his mouth with a napkin, and then leaned back in the booth with a big ass grin. "Holy shit, I never even suspected. That's some secret, bro. No wonder you've been torn up for the past few years. Denying who you are sucks the soul out of you."

He blinked. "You understand?"

"I'm surprised, but of course I understand. Did you really think otherwise?" Rome cursed when he saw the truth on his face. "You actually thought I'd have a problem with you being a sub. When the love of my life is one? And Rick's?"

Rafe rubbed his face to hide the sudden heat of embarrassment. "Figured it'd be different when you heard a man was a sub. Kind of odd, don't you think?"

Rick shook his head, his voice tinged with anger. "No, I don't. I see it all the time. I may not swing that way, but I respect the hell out of a man who knows who he is and goes after it. Tara and Sloane are some of the strongest, kickass women we know. Just because they're subs in the bedroom doesn't mean they're weak. It's quite the opposite. That's basic 101 in BDSM. Figured you'd know that already."

Relief poured true and clear from the core of his body. He couldn't help the silly grin spreading across his face as he looked at the two men he loved and respected the most in the world. "Thanks, guys. I appreciate the support."

"How are you going to get Summer back?" Rick asked.

"I've been checking out Chains because she mentioned that club to me. Seems she just joined as a member. I have a plan, but I may need your help. Do you know anyone over there?"

Rick nodded. "Yeah, my friend Dan is a member. Let me get the details and I'll get you in. You'll need to complete an orientation though and fill out a bunch of forms."

"I'll do it. I'm tired of hiding who I am and pretending. And I want you to meet her."

His brothers shared a grin. "FANTA-C strikes again, huh? I think it's time to get Remington's ass down to Vegas. The last time I talked to him, he sounded like crap. I think he broke off another relationship."

Their youngest brother had never really gotten over his childhood sweetheart, and seemed unable to find someone to love. He was still working in Atlantic City, but once Rafe moved, his brother seemed a bit more interested in making a big change.

Rick clapped him on the shoulder. "We can't wait to meet her, Rafe. Sloane and Tara will be thrilled to add another friend to their group."

"Let's just hope the odds are still in my favor. I have a lot of begging to do." Rafe stood from the booth.

Rome winced. "Bet you'll have a sore ass by the time she's done punishing you for letting her walk in the first place. Glad I'm not you, bro. Let me start making calls."

As his brother flipped out his cell phone, Rafe prepared to win the biggest dare of his life.

Chapter Eleven

*"S*UMMER, THE SCENE is ready for you. But I have a new sub out front who insists he needs to speak with you."

Her brow wrinkled in confusion. "Okay. Give me two minutes and send him in."

She finished lacing her spiked boots and adjusted her corset. She may still be uncomfortable in bondage, but the club let her go slow, at her own pace, and gave her enough men to pick from to try different things. As she prepared for her first small, public scene, her heart mourned the only man she ached for. The one who'd left almost a month ago.

Rafe Steele.

Agony speared her gut. She dreamt of him constantly, waking up with her hips bucking to empty air, and a wound in her soul that refused to heal. She understood his limits and respected his decision, but it didn't help the longing that choked her when she stared at another man in handcuffs, waiting to obey her. Hopefully, she'd eventually meet someone she could share her days and nights with—a soul mate. But for now, she took it day by day with only one name hovering on the edge of her lips.

She shook her head to clear her thoughts and brought herself under control. She'd already decided on her choice for the display with a young man she felt she could help, but had no idea who'd want to see her so close to show time.

The door opened and she stared at the entrance with curiosity.

Her heart plummeted with wrenching speed. The image of her dreams stood before her, and she practically choked on her own saliva. His naked chest sported a swirl of dark hair over rich olive skin. He stood with his bare feet spread apart, a tiny black scrap of fabric covering his impressive cock. A raw, pulsing need flooded her and left her shaking. She swallowed hard, and raised her chin high. His dark gaze delved into hers with an intensity that ripped away her breath. She forced herself to speak, the words a husky whisper. "What are you doing here?"

"I'm here for you, Summer. I'm here to make things right."

Hope rose, but she battled it back, afraid to get hurt again. "No, you weren't ready for this." She swept her hands in the air. "I can't make you be someone you don't want to be."

"The only man I want to be is the one who owns you just as much as you own me."

"Rafe—"

"Permission to speak, Mistress."

The title fell from his lips and she gasped. Her pussy clenched, and tears pricked her eyes. The strength and courage it took for him to find her and reveal himself deserved her full attention. "Permission granted," she whispered.

He closed the distance between them and knelt before her. "This isn't about getting attached to the first woman who introduced me to this lifestyle. And it isn't about trying to change who I am, or you, so it fits some ridiculous concept of what society thinks are acceptable. This is about how I feel when I'm with you. You wrecked my world. I tried to go back to what I considered normal, but I'm tired of being an empty shell. Give me another chance. I want to take you to meet my brothers and their girlfriends. I want to court you with silly flowers, and take you to the movies and share popcorn. I want to hear your dreams and your nightmares, and submit to you in the bedroom. I want to stand before anyone who will listen and tell them you're the love of my life. You took part of my soul, and I need it back." His gaze glittered with fierceness. "I dare you, Mistress."

"Dare me to what?"

He smiled. "Allow me to take the place of your submissive tonight in the public scene. To claim you as my Mistress."

She closed her eyes against the tears and the joy, shuddering with want and need for the man who knelt by her feet. Pulling him upward, she drew his head down for a kiss.

His lips took hers, the musky, spicy flavor of male desire swamping her senses. His tongue slipped into her mouth and took everything she had. In that moment, she submitted to him as sweetly as he did to her.

"I accept your dare," she murmured against his lips. "I missed you so much. Love you so much. Are you sure you're ready for this?"

"I trust you'll take care of me."

"I will." She nipped his lower lip playfully. "You do have a punishment due for leaving, though. This will be the perfect time to introduce you to the whip."

He flinched, but she caught the wild excitement in his eyes. "That's what my brothers warned me about."

"You told them everything?"

"Yes. I want you night and day, Summer Preston. No more secrets."

"You have me, Rafe Steele."

She'd won the dare of a lifetime.

Love.

Jennifer's Playlist

Wonderland – Taylor Swift

Downtown – Macklemore & Ryan Lewis

Animals – Maroon 5

Gett Off - Prince

I Know You – Skylar Grey

Heaven Help Me – Rob Thomas

Want tovWant Me -

Good For You – Selena Gomez
iTunes

Use Somebody – Kings of Leon

Wild Wild Love - Pitbull

Books by Jennifer Probst

THE STEELE BROTHERS SERIES
Catch Me
Play Me
Dare Me
Beg Me
Reveal Me

THE BILIONAIRE BUILDERS SERIES
Everywhere and Every Way
Any Time, Any Place
All or Nothing at All

SEARCHING FOR SERIES
Searching for Someday
Searching for Perfect
Searching for Beautiful
Searching for Always
Searching for Disaster

MARRIAGE TO A BILLIONAIRE
The Marriage Bargain
The Marriage Trap
The Marriage Mistake
The Marriage Merger

1001 DARK NIGHTS
Somehow, Some Way: A Billionaire Builders Novella
Searching for Mine: A Searching For Novella

About the Author

Jennifer Probst is the New York Times, USA Today, and Wall Street Journal bestselling author of both sexy and erotic contemporary romance. She was thrilled her novel, The Marriage Bargain, was the #6 Bestselling Book on Amazon for 2012. Her first children's book, Buffy and the Carrot, was co-written with her 12 year old niece, and her short story, "A Life Worth Living" chronicles the life of a shelter dog. She makes her home in New York with her sons, husband, two rescue dogs, and a house that never seems to be clean. She loves hearing from all readers! Stop by her website at http://www.jenniferprobst.com for all her upcoming releases, news and street team information.

Made in the USA
Monee, IL
01 November 2020